P9-ELV-164

Parent's Introduction

We Both Read is the first series of books designed to invite parents and children to share the reading of a story by taking turns reading aloud. This "shared reading" innovation, which was developed with reading education specialists, invites parents to read the more complex text and storyline on the left-hand pages. Then, children can be encouraged to read the right-hand pages, which feature less complex text and storyline, specifically written for the beginning reader.

Reading aloud is one of the most important activities parents can share with their child to assist them in their reading development. However, We Both Read goes beyond reading *to* a child and allows parents to share the reading *with* a child. *We Both Read* is so powerful and effective because it combines two key elements in learning: "modeling" (the parent reads) and "doing" (the child reads). The result is not only faster reading development for the child, but a much more enjoyable and enriching experience for both!

You may find it helpful to read the entire book aloud yourself the first time, then invite your child to participate in the second reading. In some books, a few more difficult words will first be introduced in the parent's text, distinguished with **bold lettering**. Pointing out, and even discussing, these words will help familiarize your child with them and help to build your child's vocabulary. Also, note that a "talking parent" icon ☺ precedes the parent's text and a "talking child" icon ☺ precedes the child's text.

We encourage you to share and interact with your child as you read the book together. If your child is having difficulty, you might want to mention a few things to help them. "Sounding out" is good, but it will not work with all words. Children can pick up clues about the words they are reading from the story, the context of the sentence, or even the pictures. Some stories have rhyming patterns that might help. It might also help them to touch the words with their finger as they read, to better connect the voice sound and the printed word.

Sharing the *We Both Read* books together will engage you and your child in an interactive adventure in reading! It is a fun and easy way to encourage and help your child to read—and a wonderful way to start them off on a lifetime of reading enjoyment!

Lulu's Wild Party

A We Both Read® Book

Text Copyright © 2008 by Paula Blankenship
Illustrations Copyright © 2008 by Larry Reinhart
All rights reserved

We Both Read® is a trademark of Treasure Bay, Inc.

Published by
Treasure Bay, Inc.
P.O. Box 119
Novato, CA 94948 USA

Printed in Singapore

Library of Congress Catalog Card Number: 2008922567

Hardcover ISBN: 978-1-60115-231-2
Paperback ISBN: 978-1-60115-232-9

We Both Read® Books
Patent No. 5,957,693

Visit us online at:
www.webothread.com

PR 11-14

Lulu's
Wild Party

By Paula Blankenship

Illustrated by Larry Reinhart

TREASURE BAY

Doorbell rings with a ding dong ding.
Birthday voices begin to sing.
Momma's in the kitchen—shake and bake.
Momma's making Lulu a . . .

. . . **birthday** cake!

Lots of gifts, and a lot of toys,
Happy girls and some bouncing boys,
Marching through the meadow—bright and bold!
Come to Lulu's party! She's six years . . .

. . . old!

Belle the butterfly squeals and shouts!
Sam the spider's a big bug scout.
Gary is a hopper—he plays ball.
Marvin likes to skate, but he hates . . .

. . . to fall!

Belle calls out, with a twist and twirl,
"Let's play games with the birthday girl!"
Music starts to play—a trumpet blares.
Everybody gathers for musical . . .

. . . chairs!

"Marvin wins!" Belle and Sam exclaim.
Let's all go play another game!
How about a game of hide and seek?
Lulu's favorite hiding place is near . . .

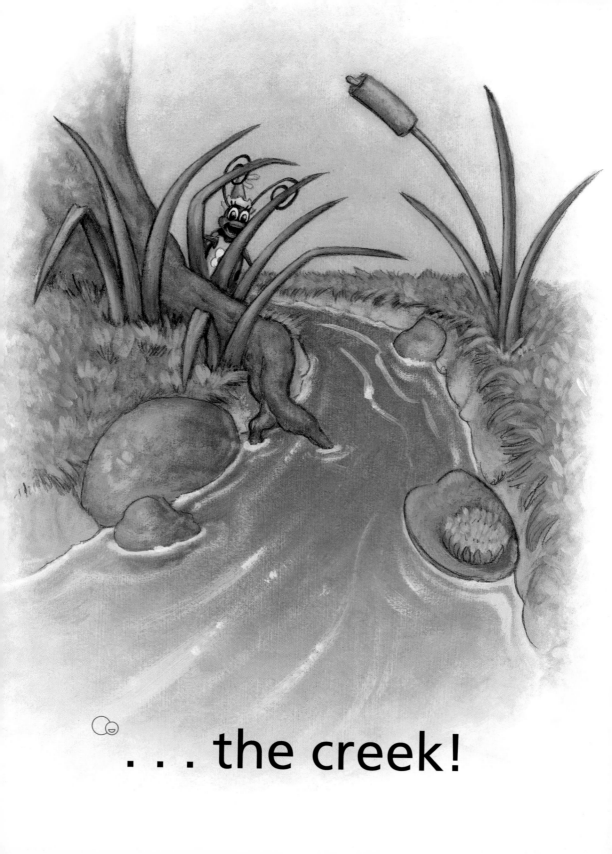

. . . the creek!

Clouds roll in and they hide the sun.
Falling rain might just spoil the fun!
Gary starts to worry about the sky.
Sammy is unhappy and Marvin may . . .

. . . cry!

Gary frowns and he must complain!
Belle just stomps and shouts, "No, not **rain**!"
Lulu just laughs as she skips and hops.
Opening her mouth for the big . . .

. . . rain drops!

"Come on guys! We can catch the breeze!
Grab a daisy and follow please!"
Everyone is happy, in the shower.
Flying through the air on their very own . . .

. . . flower!

Belle and Sam and a friendly bee
Dance about in a sweet plum tree.
Calling from above to down below,
Lulu's shouting out with a . . .

. . . big hello!

Lulu grins with a face so cute,
Holds a leaf like a parachute.
Balanced on a plum so carefully,
Lulu takes a leap off the big . . .

. . . tall tree!

"Let's have fun!" little Lulu screams.
"Splash in puddles and jump the streams!"
Racing in the rainstorm, lickety-split,
Gary starts to play in a big . . .

. . . mud pit!

Sam finds twigs from a nice peach tree.
Sam makes Lulu a water ski.
Look at all her tricks, now see her whirl!
Everybody claps . . .

. . . for the
birthday girl!

Friends all cheer, as they see her ski.
Lulu laughs and is filled with glee!
Landing on the shoreline—slip and slide,
Lulu meets an earthworm . . .

. . . and gets a ride!

Belle rides too with her hands up high.
Sam is eager and wants to try!
Gary is on *two* worms—Fred rides *one*.
Everyone is having . . .

. . . a lot of fun!

Belle stops riding and shouts out loud,
"No more rain and there's no more cloud!"
Everyone rejoices—"Hip hooray!"

Showers from the trees wash the . . .

. . . mud away!

Now we're clean and it's time to go.
Sam has something he wants to show!
Rolling on a lemon—right on top,
Sammy keeps on spinning! He just can't . . .

. . . stop!

"Let me try!" all the others shout.
They start rolling and spin about.

Racing down the hillside—what a crash!
Lemons are all squished and the juice goes . . .

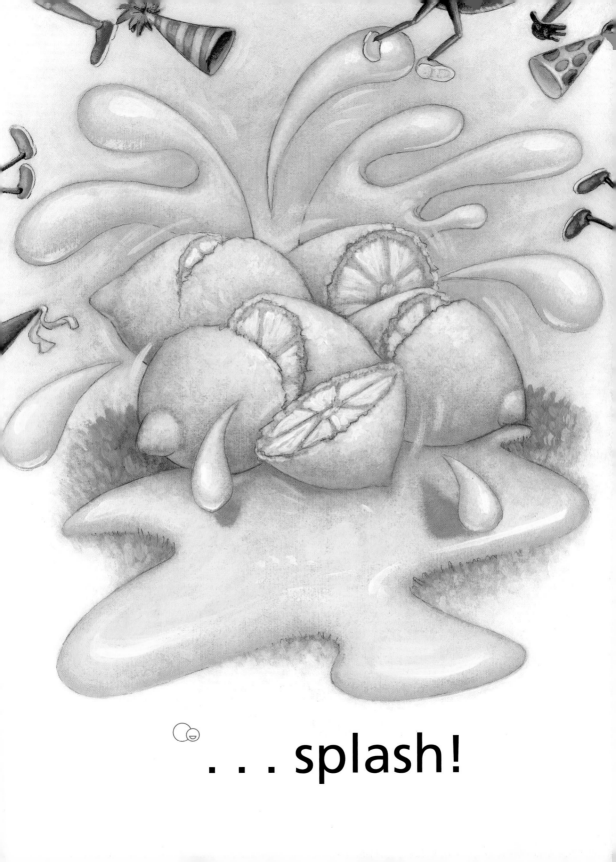

. . . splash!

Look at Lulu—at what she's made!
She's turned lemons into lemonade!
When life gives you rain, don't accept defeat!
Turn a rainy day into something . . .

. . . sweet!

Mom lights candles on Lulu's cake.
Bugs all wonder what wish she'll make!
"You can do it, Lulu!" her friends all shout.
Lulu takes a breath and she blows . . .

. . . them out!

Gifts are open and games are done.
All the bugs have had so much fun.
Lulu gets a lift and a big "Hooray!"
Another **great** birthday—another . . .

If you liked **Lulu's Wild Party,** here is another
We Both Read® Book you are sure to enjoy!

Lulu's Lost Shoes

It is time for Lulu to be off to school, but she can't
find her shoes! All her little bug friends get off the
school bus to help her find them. Now everyone
is late, the frolicking searchers are messing up the
house, and mother Ladybug is not very happy!
Featuring a lot of humor and a common situation
that all children can identify with, this book for the
very beginning reader is sure to be shared again
and again!

To see all the We Both Read books that are available,
just go online to **www.webothread.com**